PLANET DOOM

Anne Schraff

PAGETURNERS

SUSPENSE
Boneyard
The Cold, Cold Shoulder
The Girl Who Had Everything
Hamlet's Trap
Roses Red as Blood

DETECTIVE
The Case of the Bad Seed
The Case of the Cursed Chalet
The Case of the Dead Duck
The Case of the Wanted Man
The Case of the Watery Grave

ADVENTURE
A Horse Called Courage
Planet Doom
The Terrible Orchid Sky
Up Rattler Mountain
Who Has Seen the Beast?

SCIENCE FICTION
Bugged!
Escape from Earth
Flashback
Murray's Nightmare
Under Siege

MYSTERY
The Hunter
Once Upon a Crime
Whatever Happened to
    Megan Marie?
When Sleeping Dogs Awaken
Where's Dudley?

SPY
A Deadly Game
An Eye for an Eye
I Spy, e-Spy
Scavenger Hunt
Tuesday Raven

Development and Production: Laurel Associates, Inc.

SADDLEBACK
EDUCATIONAL PUBLISHING
www.sdlback.com

ISBN-13: 978-1-56254-184-2
ISBN-10: 1-56254-184-6
eBook: 978-1-60291-227-4

Printed in the United States of America
16 15 14 13 12   3 4 5 6 7 8 9 10

CONTENTS

Chapter 1

Who would ever forget the night the amusement park burned down? Its grand opening had been just one week away! Reggie Daniels and his girlfriend, Joanna Peck, had been high school students then. Now, more than two years later, they were both working and taking courses at city college.

Like everybody else, Reggie and Joanna had heard the sirens and seen the wild flames dancing hundreds of feet into the air. The smoke poured into the sky, blotting out the moon and the stars. For a while neighbors feared that half the city would burn, but the fire department did a good job. They even saved many of the buildings within the park, but the park had never opened.

Now, on a Saturday night date, Reggie and Joanna stared again at the ruins behind the ugly plywood walls. Big black NO ADMITTANCE signs were plastered all over them.

"Why don't they just tear the whole mess down and build something else here?" Joanna complained. For sure, the burned skeleton of the amusement park was now an awful eyesore in the neighborhood.

"Pop says they want to raze the place and build a shopping center," Reggie said. "So far, though, nobody is coming up with enough cash. Everybody's offering chump change."

Five years ago, everything had been different. Eddie Scott, a kid from the neighborhood, had made it big in baseball. He was a phenom who got drafted by an American League team and signed to a million-dollar contract. Eddie was the only kid from these mean streets to ever have such fabulous luck in *any* field. He was so grateful that he decided to help his neighborhood by building a state-of-the-art amusement park. He called it *Planet Doom* because it had an outer space theme. But then the fire had broken out, and all his dreams had gone up in smoke. Eddie's career soon went up in smoke, too. After two years he was cut from the team, and he vanished like a rock in deep water.

* * *

Joanna peered through a narrow crack between two pieces of plywood. "It looks so weird in there in the moonlight. I can still see the Ferris wheel and the roller coaster. Sure would've been a fun place to go if they'd gotten it up and running."

"My buddy, Erik, says there's a curse on the place," Reggie said. "That's why nothing worked out." Reggie laughed and made spooky sounds, mimicking the ghost who maybe roamed through the deserted park.

Joanna poked Reggie playfully in the ribs. "Oh, go on! There's no curse. Some fool probably just tossed a cigarette in a pile of trash on a hot windy night. That's why it all went up in flames."

"I don't know," Reggie said. "I heard that some weird old dude owned this land a long time ago. They say his wife finally had enough of him and left. When she ran off, they say the old man put a curse on the house and the land. Then his house burned down. When they built the amusement park here, maybe the curse stuck."

"Oh, Reggie, stop with the curse nonsense!" Joanna said.

"Eddie Scott must have been cursed, too," Reggie continued. "Say, what's with that dude these days? After getting a million bucks to play in the majors, he has one good season and then he busts his ankle so bad that nobody can fix it. He never did play worth beans again. The poor chump *must* have been cursed.

Or maybe the guy was just a bum—who knows?"

"Just some bad luck," Joanna said. "Happens to a lot of guys. The injury healed, but he lost his momentum or his confidence or something. Look in the stats. Plenty of guys who were rookies of the year ended up in the minors, scrambling for less money than you get making burgers."

Joanna pushed at the plywood to widen the crack so she could see better. "I remember really looking forward to Planet Doom opening. It was gonna be such a huge blast! At last we'd have something really fun to do in this nowhere neighborhood. It seemed too good to be true, and I guess it was."

Suddenly the plywood gave way, and a two-foot-wide opening appeared in the fence. The space was plenty wide for somebody to slip through.

Joanna turned and grinned at Reggie. "It's only eight o'clock. I told Mom I'd be home by ten. Want to take a look around in there?"

"Sure," Reggie said. "I always wanted to take a date to a haunted amusement park."

"Oh, Reggie, will you *stop* it!" Joanna laughed. "It's just some old deserted buildings and some burned-out hulks."

When they had squeezed through the opening, Reggie carefully moved the plywood board back in place. He didn't want a passerby to notice the big opening and discover that someone was trespassing.

"Welcome to Planet Doom," Reggie said in a deep, ominous voice. "Here you can travel to the farthest reaches of outer space. Are you ready to encounter terrors beyond your wildest nightmares? Abandon all hope, you who enter here!"

Chapter 2

"Are you making up all of that foolishness?" Joanna giggled.

"No, I'm reading it from that rickety old sign over there," Reggie said. "That's what it says."

"You can still smell burned wood, huh?" Joanna said. "But look—a lot of the park is still standing. It's a shame they don't do something about this."

"They *did* do something," Reggie said. "They shut it all up inside a tall plywood fence."

"I mean *fix* it," Joanna groaned. "Kids have nothing to do in this neighborhood. We've got one bowling alley and a pizza parlor and nothing else but a lot of beer joints up and down this street."

"Yeah," Reggie said, "we don't even have a movie theater. We gotta go way down to the mall to see the flicks."

"Maybe you and I should start a campaign to reopen Planet Doom," Reggie went on.

"Oh, stop being a fool, Reggie!" Joanna said.

Suddenly a voice came booming out over the public address system. "Welcome to Planet Doom. How nice to see visitors on a Saturday night, even though we have not yet finished the renovation."

Joanna and Reggie almost jumped out of their skins.

"I'm getting out of here!" Reggie yelled, spinning around and looking for the loose board in the fence.

Joanna grabbed Reggie's arm. "You big baby! Some kid probably put that message on the PA system as a joke. You think we're the *first* kids who got in here? I bet plenty of kids have come in here to take a look around the place."

"I guess you're right," Reggie said. "But that voice really had me going for a minute. It was kinda funny, huh? Maybe we could leave a message for the next visitors. Let's see. . . 'Welcome to Planet Doom. Prepare to be eaten by a space octopus that is scampering toward your big toe right now!'"

"Yeah, right," Joanna giggled. "Look, there's a light burning in the old snack bar. I thought the electricity had been turned off long ago. Somebody must have rigged up a generator. Oh! And there's the hall of mirrors. Looks like it didn't burn at all."

"I bet all the mirrors are broken, though," Reggie said.

Stepping cautiously into the building, they saw that only one outside wall had been blackened by the fire. Otherwise, everything seemed to be intact, even the mirrors.

"Listen," Reggie read from a sign.

"You Earthlings are now entering the Venutian landscape. Notice that the planet rotates backward in a dense layer of clouds. Do you dare to open the mirrored door to Venus?"

The door squeaked loudly as Joanna went in.

Following her, Reggie said, "Look up there. I bet that's the machine that spewed out vapor to look like the cloud cover of Venus. How could the poor fools stumbling around in here see where they were going?" he laughed.

Joanna and Reggie walked down a hallway. They bumped into several false doors because of the mirrored walls. Then, suddenly, the floor beneath their feet started rolling backward. Looking down, they saw that they had been walking on something like a level escalator—but now it had begun to rapidly move backward!

"Whoa!" Reggie shouted, stumbling and landing on all fours. Then Joanna lost her balance and fell, too.

"On the planet Venus," a strange, disembodied voice boomed out, "there is a backward rotation. Perhaps you don't remember being told that in the beginning. Alas, it seems that you did not listen."

Joanna and Reggie finally regained their feet. They turned around, facing the direction in which the floor moved. Then a wheezing sound came from overhead, and the room filled up with white clouds. It was impossible to see.

"Man!" Reggie cried. "The vapor machine still works! This ain't funny anymore, Joanna! This is *weird*. We gotta get out of here!"

The disembodied voice boomed out again. "Ah, I suppose I should have told you. There is no life on Venus. The Venutian atmosphere is very hostile to all life forms—especially to human life forms . . . human life forms . . . human life forms . . ."

Chapter 3

"I feel like I'm choking," Reggie gasped, clutching his throat.

"It's your imagination, Reggie," Joanna insisted. "Come on, grab my hand. Let's go this way."

When they came into the next room, the thick vapor had disappeared. They were facing an entire wall painted in three-dimensional landscapes of Venus. The planet's rounded mountains seemed to stretch into infinity. Reggie and Joanna felt as if they could walk right into the desertlike terrain of the jungle setting beyond.

Then the strange deep voice filled the room again. "In 1918, a great Nobel prize–winning physicist, Swvante Arrhenius, discovered that Venus had a hot, jungle atmosphere. Arrhenius said the planet was home to primeval monsters of the most awesome kind. . . ."

Suddenly, across the landscape before them, strange and hideous creatures appeared. They were tall beings, sheathed in gray-green fur. Each of their swollen heads was dominated by one pulsating red eye.

"*Reggieeeee!*" Joanne screamed. The creatures seemed to be emerging from the wall and coming toward them.

"It's trick photography," Reggie said, "there has to be a movie projector behind us."

Then the normal lighting came back on and the voice said, "We hope you have enjoyed your visit to the mysterious planet of Venus."

"There's the exit!" Joanna yelled, bounding toward it.

The pair ran outside into the cool night air. The bright stars above them and the sound of a jet airliner on its way to the airport reminded them they were back in the real world.

"Wow, what a ride!" Reggie said. "It was really cool, huh?"

Joanna giggled. "Yeah, it was. And we didn't even have to pay for it. Man, I was scared out of my wits! That was just about the coolest thrill ride I ever took. What a shame they can't reopen the park so other kids could enjoy it, too. It was so fun!"

"Yeah, *now* you say it was fun—but you were freaking out in there, Joanna," Reggie teased.

"So were you! You imagined you were choking!" Joanna said.

"I sure wish there was a food machine around here," Reggie grumbled. "I'm starving."

"You ate almost half a pizza at the bowling alley," Joanna said.

"That was two hours ago, girl! I sure would like one of those great big nutty, butterscotch-chocolate candy bars about now," Reggie said. "You don't think there's anything in that machine over there, do you?"

"Yeah, right!" Joanna said. "This place burned two years ago, remember? The doughnuts in that machine would have turned to stone by now. The candy bars would be cement. One bite would break a tooth for sure!"

Reggie shrugged and fished in his pocket for some change. "Wouldn't hurt just to *look* at the machine. Maybe the ghosts have maintenance men come in once in a while to stock it up."

The machine *looked* normal. Candy bars, little bags of nuts, and other snacks were still displayed behind the small glass windows. Reggie stuffed in 75 cents and pushed the button next to a chocolate-covered pecan bar. It dropped into the tray with a thud.

"The rock has landed!" Joanna laughed. "Look, a granite candy bar, yum, yum!" Joanna screamed. "That must be *so* disgusting by now! It has to be petrified!"

Reggie bit into the candy bar. "No, it's good. It tastes just great—like the kind I get at the machines at my job." Reggie worked as a mechanic's helper at a new car dealer. At night he took classes in automotive repair and computers.

"You're kidding me!" Joanna cried. "You mean they really last that long?"

Reggie broke off a piece of the candy bar and offered it to Joanna. "Here, try it."

"No way! I know what a human garbage disposal you are! Even *rotten* stuff tastes good to you, Reggie!" Joanna teased.

They moved on toward a ride that took passengers up in a little plane. The flames had burned off one wing, and now the lopsided wreck sat amid a tall pile of rubble.

Reggie drew closer to the plane. "Hey, that's the kind of plane my grandpa piloted," he said. "I've seen pictures."

"Too bad it burned in the fire," Joanna said.

"Hey!" Reggie yelled. "I just saw a guy up there in the cockpit!"

"Oh, come on, Reggie! It was just a shadow," Joanna scoffed.

"No, I'm *sure* I saw someone—it was an older guy," Reggie insisted.

"Maybe they put a dummy in the plane, like they do at the car museum." Joanna craned her neck. "I don't see any guy in the plane, Reggie."

"Well, I sure *thought* I saw him," Reggie said, although he now seemed much less certain.

"Hey, there's the little museum dedicated to Eddie Scott," Joanna said. "It's blackened on the outside, but it still might be okay on the inside. Let's go have a look."

When they entered the museum, the sound system narration went on.

"Welcome to the new Eddie Scott memorabilia museum. This exhibit is dedicated in gratitude to a fine young man from this neighborhood whose baseball career has made Planet Doom possible for the enjoyment of all, especially the young people."

"Look, here are pictures of Eddie when he was a Little Leaguer," Joanna said. "I was a little kid when he was getting out of high school. He was a real big shot to all of us. He took our high school to the championship."

"How old do you think Eddie Scott is by now?" Reggie wondered.

"Well, he got that million dollar contract when he was *your* age, Reggie. I'm guessing he must be about twenty-five," Joanna said. "I remember an article about him right after the park burned. The headline really stuck in my mind: *Amusement Park Dream, Like Scott's Career, Goes Up in Flames.*"

"Wow, musta really hurt the man to

read a headline like that," Reggie said.

"I guess," Joanna said as they walked from the museum. "Hey, look! There's the Mars ride. I wonder if that's as much fun as the Venus ride was."

"Well, the price is still right," Reggie laughed. "Come on. Be my guest."

Joanna and Reggie opened the door to the Mars ride and found it was brilliant red inside. "Hey, these little red cars look like real rocket ships," Reggie said. "Let's get in one of them and see where it goes!"

Chapter 4

Joanna glanced at her watch. "It's only a quarter to nine. We've got plenty of time. Yeah, let's do it!"

They each climbed into a rocket car and tightened the straps over their laps as the instructions said. Joanna was in the car right behind Reggie.

"Welcome to the Martian world," the deep voice said over the public address system. "Mars is very much like Earth. More than a hundred years ago it was said that a drought was threatening all life on Mars. The Martians sent pleas for help to Earth. Unfortunately, however, the Earthlings did not respond."

Then the rocket cars started to move down a hallway. Here, Martian landscapes—red and harsh and lifeless—lined the walls. Then they came into a great circular room where giant three-dimensional pictures of Martian landscapes appeared all around them.

"There's a robot!" Reggie shouted. He pointed to a human-sized robot clad in a silvery space suit. The robot had a huge bubble head, but its facial features were strangely unclear.

"Reggie!" Joanna cried. "It *really is* a robot—and it's coming toward us!"

Reggie laughed a hollow laugh. "Hey, cool! A real robot. Hi, robot, what's your name?"

"*My name is X7*," the robot said in a metallic monotone. "*I am a Mars expedition robot!*"

"He answered you!" Joanna gasped in surprise. "I didn't think robots answered questions."

"Nah, he's programmed to say stuff like that. I bet everybody asks him his name. Hey, stupid robot, what does this ride do? So far it's pretty boring. The Venus ride was a lot better."

Immediately there was a roar of engines, a meshing of gears, and the rocket cars whirled into motion. The cars began spinning around the room. At first it was exciting, but the little cars kept going faster and faster until Joanna and Reggie were dizzy.

"*Stop!*" Joanna screamed. She felt all over the car for an emergency button that might stop the ride. "Boy, am I getting sick! I'm so dizzy I could throw up!"

Then suddenly, the rocket cars began to slow, at last coming to a jolting standstill. The robot rolled close to their cars and spoke to them. *"I have four questions for you Earthlings. If you give the right answers, you will win a lifetime pass to Planet Doom."*

"Stupid robot, we don't want a lifetime pass. We just want out of here," Reggie snarled, yanking at the seat belts. But he soon discovered that the belts were locked. Reggie couldn't get out of the car!

"Question number 1:" intoned the robot. *"Are you a baseball fan?"*

"Yeah," Reggie said. "So what?"

"Your answer has been recorded. Question number 2: Do you know who Eddie Scott is?"

"Yeah, he's the chump who paid for this stupid park," Reggie snapped.

"Your answer has been recorded. Question number 3: Do you think it was fair of the team manager to cut Eddie Scott after just two seasons?" asked the robot.

"Sure," Reggie said. "The guy was a total bum."

"Your answer has been recorded. Question number 4: Should Eddie Scott be given another chance in the majors?" the robot asked.

Reggie laughed out loud. "I wouldn't let that guy play for my Little League club. Everyone remembers his final games here—*el stinko.*"

"I am sorry to say you have not given the correct answers," the robot said flatly. *"You have not won the lifetime pass to Planet Doom. Instead, you will soon be departing on the subterranean ride."*

"Hey, maybe *that's* cool," Reggie said hopefully.

"How about me?" Joanna asked. "Don't I get to come, too?"

But Joanna's rocket car remained in place as Reggie's car zoomed ahead on the track. Reggie hadn't gone 10 feet before he was drenched in water. In a few seconds, the water came up to his chest. *"Hey!"* he screamed. "You can't do this to me! It's illegal to build a ride where a guy almost gets drowned!" He didn't know what he was yelling at, but he was mad. He thought that whoever designed this ride must have been insane to think that it would be fun.

"Reggie! Are you all right?" Joanna screamed after him. "What's going on down there?"

"I'm soaking wet, and I want to get out of this slimy water," Reggie yelled. "Yuk! It looks like swamp water, and it *smells* like swamp water, too!"

Then the deep voice rang out. *"You are now on Mars as it might have been, long, long ago. This was a time when Mars was blessed with plenty of water. There were plentiful forms of microscopic life then, perhaps even insects. Soon you will encounter great diving beetles, water lice, water scorpions, and even small snakes."*

"Hey!" Reggie shrieked. "Get me out of here. Now the water's full of ugly, creepy stuff!" He was being attacked by dozens of creatures swimming up to his chin. Then, suddenly, the rocket car zoomed up the ramp and returned to the room where Joanna was.

Reggie waved his arms wildly, knocking small, shiny creatures out of his hair and clothing.

"Wait until I get out of here! I'm telling everybody what's going on in this horrible place," Reggie threatened.

The robot slid over toward Joanna. It asked her the same question it had first asked Reggie. *"Question number 1: Are you a baseball fan?"*

"No!" Joanna cried. She had no intention of going down below with the diving beetles and the water lice!

Suddenly, the seat belts in both rocket cars disconnected. Joanna and Reggie leaped out and turned back the way they had come.

"Let's find the quickest way out to the street," Reggie said.

"Yeah," Joanna said. "I think it's this way. We'll try to backtrack the way we came."

"Man, I had no idea those stupid, dangerous rides were still in working order," Reggie cried out as they raced toward the fence. "I can't figure it out. Just wait'll we tell the cops how dangerous this place is. I coulda *drowned* down there! The cops will get on this

"Come on!" Reggie said. "That's too weird! Hey, let's see if there's a back door in this building that leads to the street. I just want to get back in the real world!"

"You said it!" Joanna agreed, hanging on to Reggie's arm so tightly that her fingers ached. "I can't wait to tell everyone what happened to us here. This isn't just some innocent, harmless old ruin of an amusement park. It's really a dangerous place!"

"Yeah, but we gotta get out of here first," Reggie said.

Joanna nodded. "Let's get going!"

"Look, there's a door. Maybe it leads outside," Reggie said. "We just need to get back to the plywood fence. We don't have to go out the way we came in. I'll kick down a board if we can just get to any part of the fence."

Joanna opened the door and peeked out into the darkness. There was no sign of the robot.

fast. This place is a real hazard, man!"

"Reggie, there's still some horrible bug on your back," Joanna gasped. "*Ewww*, that one is hideous. It's got a million legs!"

"Knock it off me!" Reggie yelled.

Joanna picked up a stick and knocked the bug off.

Joining hands, Joanna and Reggie sprinted ahead in the darkness. Then they heard the loud clanking noise of turning wheels, and Joanna looked back. "Oh, no! The robot is coming after us!" she cried.

"No way!" Reggie shouted. Joanna noticed that there was real fear in Reggie's voice now. "Let's get going, Joanna. We can't let it catch us!"

Chapter 5

In a minute, Reggie and Joanna passed the burned-out old plane ride. To reach the fence, they had only about 500 yards to go.

But now the robot had a weapon. When the robot fired it, a greasy gel spewed out, covering the concrete pathway all around Joanna and Reggie. As the slippery surface forced them to slow down, the robot gained on them.

"He's right on top of us. We gotta hide somewhere!" Reggie said.

The sign on a building just ahead said *Jovian Jump.* Joanna pointed to it. "That way, Reggie. We'll hide in the Jovian Jump!"

Joanna and Reggie turned sharply, slipping and stumbling on the greasy gel. Finally, they scrambled into the large building. It was designed to look like Jupiter with a large red spot painted on the side.

Reggie and Joanna peered out a window to see if the robot had spotted them coming in here.

"I don't see the robot anywhere," Reggie said. "After all, it's just a piece of high-tech machinery. It's programmed to do amazing things, but it can't *think.* It probably just kept going down the main walkway."

"I'm not so sure, Reggie," Joanna said. "There's something *different* about that robot—like it's almost human!"

"Yeah?" Reggie asked nervously. "Like maybe it's *not* a robot? You think maybe it's some kind of ghost?"

"It could be a guy dressed up to *look* like a robot. Maybe the guy only *looks* like he's moving on wheels. Maybe he's on skates. Or maybe it *is* something from outer space," Joanna said.

"I think we're in the clear," she said. "Let's run for the fence, Reggie. I don't want to spend a minute more than we have to in this place."

Reggie and Joanna started running down the dark, deserted walkway toward the distant fence. Then, suddenly, an odd-looking figure loomed in their path. Wearing a huge, ten-gallon hat, he looked like an old-time cowboy. He were swinging a lasso as if he was herding an invisible herd of cattle. The man's face was covered by a plastic mask of a television cowboy from the 1950s.

"Howdy, young folks," he called out to Joanna and Reggie. "You leaving Planet Doom already? Why are you in such a big hurry? I betcha you ain't seen half of what we got here. What are you—a couple of tenderfeet?"

Joanna and Reggie exchanged nervous looks. "Uh, my mom is expecting me home by eleven," Joanna said politely. She thought maybe this was a crazy old homeless man who had stumbled on the abandoned amusement park and decided to call it home.

"Yeah," Reggie said, "we need to get home, Pops. It's been real nice talking to you, but we gotta be on our way now."

"I don't like it when young folks call me 'Pops'," the cowboy said sternly. "It's a way of saying, 'Get outta my way 'cause your time is past.' Modern folks tend to throw stuff away too quick. They throw *people* away, too—even when there's plenty of good left in them."

"Uh, sorry if I offended you, sir," Reggie said, "but we gotta be home by eleven, okay?"

"You look grown up enough to me," the cowboy said. "You don't look like little kids who got to be scampering home so early. Why don't you stay around for a while and have some fun?"

"Who are you, anyway?" Reggie asked. "This place has been closed for years. Where did you come from?"

"I'm from the Lazy X27 corral," said the cowboy.

This guy really *was crazy*. A cold chill went up Joanna's spine. She forced a smile to her lips. "Well, it's really nice to have met you, sir. We appreciate your invitation to stay and enjoy the park. We wish we could—but we really have to get home," she said.

"You been over to the Big League exhibit?" the cowboy asked. "It's the best thing in the park. Nobody ought to leave Planet Doom before they take a walk through the Big League exhibit."

"Next time, we'll go there first," Reggie promised. He turned to Joanna and whispered, "Take my hand and we'll make a break for it. I figure the fence can't be more than thirty yards away." Joanna nodded. Then the two of them joined hands and broke into a desperate run for the fence.

But then, with awesome skill, the cowboy spun out his lariat. It sailed over

Reggie's head, expertly dropping down and snagging his ankles. Reggie lay gasping in the dirt, his ankles tightly bound. "Hey, man, that's not funny!" he yelled. Leaning forward, Reggie tried to get the rope off his ankles. But every time he loosened the rope a bit, the cowboy yanked harder, dragging Reggie backward a few feet. Working quickly, Joanna knelt and loosened the rope just enough for Reggie to pull free. He quickly scrambled to his feet.

But then the old cowboy blew a whistle. Instantly, two huge dogs appeared at his command.

"We're going over to the Big League exhibit now," the cowboy said. "You don't want these puppies of mine to shoo you over there, do you? If they dislike you, they're likely to chew you up and spit you out along the way."

When Reggie and Joanna tried to make a move in any direction except toward the gray-domed Big League exhibit, the dogs circled, growling and snarling. Foamy white saliva was dripping from their jaws.

"We just want to go home," Joanna groaned. "We never did anything to you. Can't you just let us go home?"

"Well, you can't always do things just the way you want to, little lady," the cowboy said in an amiable voice. "Listen, you'll really get a kick out of the Big League exhibit. It's the experience of a lifetime. You don't want to miss it."

Inside the exhibit was a small playing field ringed by stadium seats, just like in a regular ballpark! All around the circular park were the kind of colorful advertisements you would see in a real stadium. But these big signs were old and faded. Reggie thought this place must have been used to teach kids how to play baseball several years ago. Maybe Eddie Scott had wanted to come back here for some reason. Maybe he had wanted to give little kids the thrill of being taught baseball by a million-dollar rookie like he was.

With his dogs right next to him, the cowboy seated himself in the bleachers near the big scoreboard.

"Play ball!" he shouted, tossing a baseball to Reggie.

Joanna stared at Reggie, who helplessly stared back. Nervously, they began tossing the ball back and forth in a game of catch. Every time Reggie or Joanna missed a catch, the old cowboy would boo and hoot. An electronic machine at his side joined him in a recorded chorus of cat calls and jeers.

"Lousy little punk!" the old cowboy screamed out. "You're a loser—nothing but a butterfingers! Get that bum outta here! Send him back to the minors! He's nothing but a no-talent wannabe."

Finally, Reggie and Joanna stopped playing. They had had enough. Reggie looked up at the cowboy.

"Okay, man, you've had your fun.

How about it? Can we go now?" he pleaded.

"Sure, get out of here!" the cowboy snorted. He grasped the collars of his two straining dogs. "Use the back entrance. Now, *git*—and good riddance to both of you!"

The frightened teenagers ran for the back door with the big red exit sign over it. Reggie grasped the door handle and swung it wide. At last they were escaping!

Chapter 6

The fence was nowhere in sight. Instead, Reggie and Joanna found themselves slipping and sliding down a steep hillside. Finally, they came to rest in a deep round pit.

The cowboy's grinning face appeared at the upper rim of the pit. "Uh-oh. Guess I forgot to tell you about the ice hole. It's another fun ride. It was supposed to have water and frozen icicles, but the fire messed up the system. There used to be a stairway running up the other side so the fun-seekers could climb out. But the ladder got lost somehow. . . ."

"Just throw us a rope, man," Reggie cried out in a desperate voice.

"Now don't get all riled up," the

cowboy said. "Why are you young folks always in such a hurry? Come on now, you kids had some fun here tonight, didn't you? Why, this amusement park was built just so kids like you would have someplace to go! It was meant to relieve the boredom of living in this rundown neighborhood. Tell me—you *did* have fun here, didn't you?"

Reggie knew that the old cowboy wanted to hear that they had a great time. He figured that if he got on the crazy old fool's good side, maybe he'd toss them a rope so they could get out of the pit. So Reggie said, "Oh, yeah, we had a lot of fun. This is really a cool place. And we're coming back soon, believe you me."

"This is the best amusement park we ever visited," Joanna joined in. "We'll come back every chance we get."

"Did you know that the city plans to tear all this down?" the cowboy asked. "They want to build a *shopping mall* here!

Can you imagine such a thing? What fun is that? For a long time, I thought they'd rebuild it as an amusement park. But now I hear they're gonna tear it all down," the old man's voice had been sad, but now it hardened with anger. "They're even gonna tear down Eddie Scott's museum. Can you *believe* that! They're gonna erase the memory of the fine young man who tried to give a little fun to the kids of his neighborhood."

"Uh, that's too bad," Reggie said.

"Liar, liar, pants on fire," the old cowboy said bitterly, a harsh insane tone coming into his voice. "You didn't think much of Eddie Scott, now did you? You were probably one of those little creeps who screamed at him and threw stuff at him when he was having a bad year. He was trying to live up to his whiz kid reputation the best he could. But guys like *you* wouldn't give him a chance. No, you were too busy throwing trash and peanut shells at him."

"Look, I hardly know who the guy was," Reggie lied. The truth was that he and his dad had gone down to the stadium for Eddie's last game. Like many others in the crowd, they had jeered when Eddie struck out for the third time that day.

"You called him a *chump* and a *bum*, kid," the cowboy hissed. "Don't think I forgot about that."

Reggie *recognized* that voice now. He looked at Joanna in horror. The old cowboy and the robot were one and the same! Whoever had been hiding in the robot suit was now hiding behind the cowboy mask. "I didn't mean that," Reggie said desperately. "I was only joking. I was *proud* of Eddie Scott for making it big. Hey, we all were. One of us getting the big bucks—"

"Yeah," Joanna chimed in. "Eddie coulda taken his money and spent it all on himself. But he built this park for the neighborhood instead. He was a great guy. He was out to help us. Man, he was the *best*."

"Sure, you say that *now*," the cowboy said bitterly, "but none of you would give him a break when he started to slip. Everybody loves a winner. When you begin to lose, you ain't got a friend in the world. All the fans turned out to be fair-weather bums. Eddie always gave his autograph to anybody who asked. But that all changed right quick. When he wasn't getting any hits, he couldn't *give* those autographed balls away."

"Did you know Eddie Scott well?" Reggie asked politely. He was still hoping that if he made pleasant conversation with the crazy old coot, the man would have a little pity on them and maybe throw down a rope.

"Yep. Went to all his games. He was always nice to me. In my time, I played baseball, too. I was never the player Eddie was, though. I was always stuck with some rinkydink little minor club.

But Eddie was real good to me. That's why I hang around here—out of respect for Eddie. I keep the generator going and the candy and snack machines stocked. I keep hoping some young folks might break through the fence the city built and come on in. When they stop at the museum, they can see all the trophies Eddie won, and appreciate the kid a little bit," the old cowboy said.

Reggie's sympathy with the sad old man had almost overcome his disgust and anger. "That's wonderful," he said. "It's really great that you're doing that," he said.

"You're not the first kids to come through. No, not hardly. But the other guys were *fans* of Eddie's. They said *nice* things about him. After they went on some of the rides, I gave them souvenirs from the museum. I could tell that they'd treasure them," the cowboy said, his voice softer.

"That would be cool, all right,"

Reggie said, "to have a memento of Eddie Scott's. Maybe after you toss us a rope you can find a little memento of Eddie for us, too."

The cowboy cackled viciously. "Oh, it's a little late for that, kid. You already made it crystal clear how *you* felt about Eddie."

"Oh, no, sir—I *told* you I was only joking. Eddie Scott was a *wonderful* guy," Reggie insisted.

After a long silence the cowboy said, "No, once you get out of here, the first thing you'll do is go to the law. You'll whine about what a bad time I gave you. You'll report my puppies. Then the police will come. There'll be TV and newspaper guys all over the place. They'll want to take pictures of the crazy old man who's been keeping the flame alive at Eddie Scott's amusement park. They'll write about that *chump* Eddie Scott and the *insane* old man. That's how the story will go. Coupla losers to laugh at. After that, they'll tear down this place and toss me in some nuthouse. Then nobody will be left to remember Eddie. *Nobody!*"

"Hey, look, we'll keep quiet," Reggie begged. "We *promise*."

"Yes, just toss us a rope and we'll be outta here, honest! As far as we're concerned, none of this ever happened," Joanna said.

The old man groaned. "Have you any idea what those newspaper and TV guys did to Eddie when he was still playing? They ridiculed him. They put cartoons in the paper making him look like a fool. They demanded that he be cut and thrown on the ash heap. In the end, they got their way. Eddie was cut. He couldn't even get a job on a minor league team. After that, he played in a dilapidated stadium in the middle of the desert," the cowboy said.

"I'm really sorry about that," Reggie said, "but *we* didn't do it. We're just kids, man—and we need to go home now. But we can't get out of this pit without some help. The walls are too steep and slippery. Please don't leave us here, man. We'll *die!*"

Chapter 7

"Well, *I'm* not gonna kill you. I don't even have a weapon," the cowboy said. "I'm afraid of guns. The only defense I have are my puppies. You want to know their names? The brown one is Homerun and the black one is Shutout. They're real good dogs. They'll do anything in the world for me. If anything bad happens to you, it ain't my fault. Oh, yes, I'm a gentle fellow. I don't even kill spiders. When a spider gets in my house, I escort it outside. No one could blame *me* if you folks fell into the pit and couldn't get out.

"People would say it was just another accident. Like when Eddie Scott broke his ankle and headed down the road to ruin. Accidents happen."

The cowboy sadly shook his head then and turned away.

"You can't *leave* us down here!" Reggie screamed. "It might be days or even weeks before anyone comes by here! You *got* to throw us a rope."

Reggie and Joanna could hear the cowboy whistling and the dogs yelping happily. But the sounds gradually grew fainter and fainter until pretty soon the only sound they could hear was the roar of a jet engine over the city.

"Reggie," Joanna cried, "what are we gonna do?"

"I don't know! How should I know? Maybe we could try crawling up again, but it's just too steep. We'd just start falling back. The walls of this place are as slippery as a wet sink!"

"But, Reggie, what if *nobody* comes? What if we're stuck down here forever?" Joanna said, her voice thick with fear.

"I don't know why we came to this stupid place anyway!" Reggie said bitterly. "The signs said 'no admittance.' Why didn't we just walk on by?" His eyes narrowed then. "*You* were the one who monkeyed with the loose board. *You* were the smart aleck who said, '*It's only eight o'clock, so why don't we just sneak in?*'" he went on in a mocking voice.

"*You* wanted to have a look as much as I did," Joanna cried. "If you didn't want to do it, we wouldn't have. Admit it—you wanted to come in, too!"

"I know, I know," Reggie said. "I'm sorry, Joanna. But how could we have been so *stupid*? That old guy is really off his rocker. He crouches in this place like a spider in a web, just waiting for unsuspecting flies like us to come by. Oh, man! If we'd just gone somewhere else tonight, we'd be home in our beds sleeping now. And tomorrow we'd wake up and have a nice breakfast. Man, I'm really starving!"

"You're thinking about food at a time like this?" Joanna cried.

"Joanna, don't you get it? We're *doomed*! Why shouldn't I be thinking of my last meal?" Reggie groaned.

"Stop talking like that! By now our folks know that something is wrong. I'm sure they're out looking for us. Before long, they'll call the police and report us missing," Joanna said.

"Yeah, right—and the cops will come directly to Planet Doom! Don't you remember, Joanna? We pushed the board back in place so nobody would see that it was disturbed!"

"*You* did that, Reggie, you idiot!" Joanna yelled. "That was really *brilliant*! If you hadn't done that, someone would see the opening and figure out we were in here!"

"But if *you* hadn't talked me into this in the first place, we wouldn't be in this mess at all," Reggie said. "None of this would have happened if you'd just kept your big mouth shut."

Joanna crumpled in a heap on the

ground. "Oh, Reggie, listen to us! We're at each other's throats like a couple of junkyard dogs. What good is it gonna do to turn on each other like this?"

"*Nothing* is gonna do us any good, Joanna. That old man is a psycho, pure and simple. He doesn't *want* us to get out of here alive. He probably came in here just after the fire and appointed himself the defender of that chump ball player's reputation. You heard him say he was a big fan of that loser. By now he figures that gives him a purpose in life. He hangs around here like the phantom of the opera. He keeps the shell of Eddie's amusement park going, and when some poor fools wander in, he gives them a few thrills and lets 'em die. I bet there are other kids' bones buried all over this place!"

"Oh, Reggie, do you *really* believe that other people have wandered in here and . . . never left?" Joanna asked, her voice trembling.

"Sure," Reggie said. "Lots of people disappear. Kids our age, especially. One day they're here and the next day they're gone. Everybody thinks they ran away, and maybe some did. But maybe not *all* of them. Maybe some of them ended up right here at Planet Doom. Remember Jimmy Wayne? He just *vanished* last spring. Maybe he wandered in here just like we did."

"Everybody said he went off to join a band," Joanna said.

"Maybe. Or *maybe* what's left of him is around here somewhere. Maybe we'll stumble over his bones—"

"*Reggie!*" Joanna gasped. "Stop talking like that!"

"And Sal. They said he got mixed up with a bad crowd. But maybe the truth is that he came to Planet Doom instead," Reggie went on grimly. "Maybe he fell into the old man's trap, too. . . ."

Chapter 8

"We *can't* just give up!" Joanna insisted. "There must be a way we can get out of here. What're these walls made of? Maybe we could chip some holes and make little footholds. Come on, Reggie, let's at least try!"

"It's no use," Reggie said. "This looks like the end of the line, babe."

"Okay for you, Reggie. Go ahead and be a quitter if you want to!" Joanna snapped. She went to the wall and began scratching at it with her nail file. When she had made a small dent, she felt encouraged. "Reggie, look—I chipped it a little! If we made footholds we could just climb out!"

Reggie glared at Joanna, but he joined her, chipping at the wall with his small penknife. After a few minutes, though, he gave up. "All we can do is make *tiny* holes. By the time we could carve out real footholds, we'd be too exhausted to use them."

"Come on, Reggie, help me!" Joanna cried. She stabbed her nail file into the wall again and again.

"We might as well just sit here and rest until we die of thirst or hunger," Reggie said. He leaned back and closed his eyes.

Joanna continued to work, kneeling on the dirt and picking at the slippery walls. But before long, even *she* had to admit that she was making almost no headway. And her knees were starting to hurt from kneeling on the hard ground.

"Look, Reggie, there are tracks over there!" she cried.

"So what?" Reggie said with a tired groan.

"Some kind of little vehicle must have traveled down here. It must have come

But the door was jammed shut. They could see that the fire had melted the hardware.

"Oh, Reggie," Joanna cried in a panicky voice, "what if there *is* no way out? What will we do? Will we have to go back to the pit?"

Reggie looked up. "I figure it's about a hundred feet up to the roof. Maybe we could crawl up to those burned rafters. But oh, man, if we fall from there. . ."

down the slide where we fell. Where did it go? It must have gone *somewhere*! Reggie, look, the tracks go over to this wall. The ride must have taken the people down the slope and then . . . Reggie! There's a door here—it *has* to lead somewhere!" Joanna shouted.

Reggie leaned hard on the white door that exactly blended in to the white, slippery walls. Eventually, it yielded. "A tunnel. It's a tunnel, Jo!"

"The little cars must have gone flying down the slope, and then disappeared into the tunnel as a part of the ride. Come on, Reggie, let's try to get out through the tunnel!"

"With our luck, it probably leads right into the old psycho's lair," Reggie said in disgust. But he went first, leading the way slowly. Since it was very dark, the two teenagers held hands so they wouldn't get separated. Along the way, they splashed through puddles of water.

"Keep moving, Reggie," Joanna

urged. "I bet this leads to a place at the fence!"

"Yeah, *right!*" Reggie muttered.

"Hurry, Reggie," Joanna cried. "Maybe the old man will look in the pit to check up on us. When he sees we're gone, he's sure to come after us."

"And sic those vicious dogs on us," Reggie added.

The tunnel turned in a wide arc. Joanna could imagine the little cars on the tracks, careening around the turn while everybody screamed in delight.

"Hey, Joanna, do you hear that weird music?" Reggie asked.

"Yeah, it's really spooky—like the music they play in those cheapo horror films just before something awful happens," Joanna said with a shudder.

"Oops," Reggie grunted as he bumped into a wall that turned out to be another door. Shoving it open, he saw a ramp leading upward. Joanna and Reggie followed the tracks until they

came to a huge room. The first thing they noticed was that its roof had been burned off in the fire. When they looked up, they could see the moon and th stars. The badly scorched walls arou them revealed colorful paintings of s planet's desolate environment. There barren desertlike scenes with st twisted vegetation. Joanna could there had once been a roller within this room. No doubt i final thrill of the ride that with a slide down the slippe

Looking at a faded, bla Reggie read the words alo to Proxima Centauri, the Earth. As you see, it i and desolate. . . ." Reg the rest of the sign burned the words av

"Now how do building?" Reggie looked around f try that door ov

Chapter 9

Reggie and Joanna continued to look around. Soon they found another door, and to their relief, it opened. It was now after one o'clock in the morning. Overhead, the moon beamed like a giant searchlight. Just seeing the big, white moon spilling light on this dark place was comforting to both of them.

Outside, with the milky moonlight shining down on them, Joanna and Reggie struggled to get their bearings. They quickly saw that they were surrounded by the skeleton-like hulks of burned buildings. This end of the park had obviously gotten the worst of the fire.

"We gotta head for the closest part of the fence. That weirdo and his dogs could be anywhere. If he sees us, we're in big trouble," Reggie said.

Holding hands, they ran through the ruins, searching for the fence. But immediately they heard the barking of the old cowboy's dogs.

"The dogs smell us," Joanna wailed. "Oh, Reggie, they sound so close!"

"*Hurry*, babe," Reggie cried, just as the dark shapes of the two dogs came roaring out of the darkness. Snarling and snapping, the big animals leaped over the debris.

"We'll never make it!" Reggie panted, as he looked around desperately. They had reached the Ferris wheel ride just as the dogs caught up to them. Joanna hopped into a car and pulled the door shut. But at the same moment a furious dog leaped against the glass, howling in frustration.

Then suddenly, the lights of the Ferris wheel blinked on, and the giant wheel began to *move*—even though some of the cars were badly burned and the entire mechanism was damaged beyond repair. As it turned, the great wheel groaned, sounding as if it were about to break at any moment.

The old cowboy then appeared, shining his flashlight up at Reggie and Joanna. Their little car had almost reached the top of the Ferris wheel now. Even in the dark, they saw that the old cowboy's mask was gone.

"Come down from there," the old man shouted. "The Ferris wheel is broken. The cars could drop at any moment. You must open the door of your car and climb down on the steel frame of the Ferris wheel."

"Yeah, sure!" Reggie screamed in reply. "Maybe get crushed by moving parts and then eaten by your dogs!"

The man rushed to the controls of the Ferris wheel. When it had been working properly, the tumbling cars had always stayed upright as the great wheel turned. But now the wheel groaned, and some of the cars turned upside down as the broken and melted pulleys and gears clanged against one another. The engine kept struggling to turn the wheel on the mangled skeleton of the superstructure. But the whining of the stressed metal grew steadily louder.

Joanna and Reggie's car stalled on the very top of the wheel. Trembling and flashing, the red, blue, and green lights on the towering ride made a lurid sight in the darkness.

"What if the car falls?" Joanna asked fearfully, staring out at the twisted metal holding the car in place.

"Let's hope—" Reggie started to say. But then the Ferris wheel began turning again. The old man had gotten it started. Now their car was moving down— nearly within the grasp of the angry old cowboy! They could see him standing below, holding a crowbar in his hand, as he waited for their car. The expression on his face was twisted and wild.

Without the smiling cowboy mask, they could see his *real* face—withered, lined, and scarred with bitterness. As he waited for their car to come down, he started swinging the crowbar like a baseball bat. . . .

Chapter 10

Then Joanna and Reggie saw fire trucks and police cars streaming into the park, their sirens screaming. Dozens of startled neighbors had made calls when they saw the lights on the Ferris wheel. Something *strange* was going on behind the plywood fence!

The man and his dogs began to run, but they were soon caught. Out of concern for his pets' safety, the old cowboy ordered the dogs to be docile. An officer from animal control took them off without harm. The police took charge of the man.

A firefighter helped Joanna and Reggie climb down from the broken Ferris wheel.

"Thank God you came—we could

have been killed!" Joanna cried gratefully.

"Man, we really thought we were goners," Reggie said.

"What were you kids doing here anyway?" a police officer asked. "Didn't you see the *no admittance* signs? This is a heckuva dangerous place."

"We were . . . stupid," Reggie said. "We thought it would be okay to just take a look behind the fence. . . ."

"Yeah," Joanna agreed, "it turned out that was a *real* stupid idea."

After Reggie and Joanna described all that had happened, a police officer drove them home. It wasn't until the following day that they made a sad discovery.

Both of the teenagers were called down to the police station to give further information about their ordeal. It was then that Police Lieutenant Tessie Jones told them, "The man who terrorized you is Ross Scott—the father of Eddie Scott, the baseball player who paid for the amusement park."

"His *father*?" Reggie gasped. "I thought he was a homeless man who had nowhere else to go. Man—*Eddie Scott's dad!* I bet Eddie will be really busted up when he finds out what his old man has been up to."

"That's why he was so ticked off when you called Eddie a chump and a bum," Joanna said. "And that's why he wanted to keep the place going—to honor his son. He was trying to be the custodian of his son's masterpiece."

"Poor old guy," Reggie said, feeling a wave of sympathy for the man who had caused them so much misery. "I guess he was really crushed when his son got kicked out of baseball. Especially after everybody in the neighborhood got their hopes up so high."

"Yeah," Joanna said, "Eddie had spent all his money on Planet Doom. Then, when it burned, he didn't have that or his career either."

"Where's Eddie Scott now?" Reggie

asked. "He's got to come down here and take care of his old man. He needs to get the old guy into a good hospital where they can help him."

Lt. Jones said, "When Eddie Scott got dropped from the majors, he tried his hand at a lot of jobs. He even worked as a handyman for a while—but nothing panned out for him. He had blown all his security on the amusement park, and pretty soon he was living on the street. From time to time, we'd pick him up and dry him out. Eddie was drinking pretty heavily by that time. He was really a sad case."

"Oh, man," Reggie said, "and now this. . . ."

"Eddie is feeling no pain now," Lt. Jones said. "On one of those really cold, rainy nights we had last January, Eddie Scott was sleeping under some newspapers in an alley. Somebody noticed him and called the paramedics— but by that time he wasn't sleeping anymore. He had died of exposure. Eddie Scott was only twenty-five years old when he died. The cops, we took up a collection to bury him. . . ."

Joanna looked at Reggie, with tears welling up in her eyes. Then she turned to Lt. Jones. "How could such a thing happen? How could something so awful happen to a guy who had it all?" she asked in a soft voice.

"I guess he never got his skills back after the injury," Lt. Jones said. "My husband and I used to go to the games. At the end, he was really bringing the team down. People would cuss him out and throw peanuts and hamburger cartons at him. It just wore him down. Just imagine doing your job as best you can while sixty thousand people are cussing you out for not being good enough. Imagine *sixty thousand* people who hate your guts, just because you've disappointed them."

Joanna slipped her hand into

Reggie's. "I hope when they build over Planet Doom, they leave something of Eddie Scott's in place—maybe the little museum or something. Everybody should remember that he tried to do something nice for the people in his old neighborhood," she said.

Reggie nodded. He stared over at the Ferris wheel, now dark, as it loomed over the neighborhood. "Maybe we could get a little petition going," he said, "so there would at least be a little plaque in the new mall. Something that says Eddie Scott was a good-hearted guy."

Joanna gave Reggie a hug. "Good idea. I'll start it going," she promised.

Just about everybody in the whole neighborhood signed the petition—even Jimmy Wayne and Sal—who, as it turned out, had only run away to chase a dream for a while. And one day a few months later, there was a big bronze plaque at the entrance to the brand new mall, which was named Eddie Scott Plaza.

COMPREHENSION QUESTIONS

RECALL

1. Why was the amusement park surrounded by an ugly plywood fence?

2. Why had Planet Doom been built in a down-and-out neighborhood?

3. Who offered Reggie and Joanna a lifetime pass to Planet Doom? What would they have to do to get it? Where were they at this time?

CAUSE AND EFFECT

1. What caused Reggie to become so uncomfortable and afraid when he took the Mars ride?

2. What did the old cowboy do that caused Reggie to fall to the ground?

VOCABULARY

1. The old cowboy called Reggie a "no talent *wannabe*." What's a *wannabe*?

2. The old cowboy said that Eddie Scott had been *ridiculed* by TV and newspaper reporters. What does *ridiculed* mean?

3. The old cowboy's dogs were named *Homerun* and *Shutout*. In baseball, what does *shutout* mean?

ANALYZING CHARACTERS

1. Which character in the story could be described as *deranged*? Explain your thinking.

2. Which character tried harder to get out of the pit? Give an example.